John W. Hile

Plans for Constructing the Improved Hammonton Incubators

also information on incubation and appliances

John W. Hile

Plans for Constructing the Improved Hammonton Incubators
also information on incubation and appliances

ISBN/EAN: 9783337380779

Printed in Europe, USA, Canada, Australia, Japan

Cover: Foto ©Andreas Hilbeck / pixelio.de

More available books at **www.hansebooks.com**

PLANS FOR CONSTRUCTING

THE

IMPROVED HAMMONTON

INCUBATORS

ALSO INFORMATION ON

Incubation and Appliances.

——BY——

J. W. HILE,

VALLEY FALLS, KAN.

REVISED EDITION, PRICE 25 Cts.

DES MOINES:
IOWA PRINTING COMPANY,
1888.

INDEX

PREFACE.

My object in revising my little book is,

1st. To correct typographical errors which appeared in the first edition.

2nd. To enlarge.

3d. To simplify the directions for constructing the Incubators.

4th. To give clearer ideas and more information on Incubation and appliances.

5th. To make the book a favorite among poultry breeders in general, feeling confident it fills a want which has long been felt by thousands who have been anxiously looking for a more practical Incubator and more practical instructions on Incubation, than has heretofore been offered to the public.

It is not unusual to find articles in various journals condemning artificial incubation, written by egotistical men of limited experience, who have tried one, two or three fraud Incubators, and found artificial Incubators to be a failure (?).

The practicability of artificial incubation is no longer a question with men of experience. The question is, what make of Incubators will do the best work?　　　　　J. W. HILE.

ARTIFICIAL INCUBATION.

Failures in hatching with Incubators are generally due to the following causes:

1st. Irregular heat.

2d. Too much heat under the eggs.

3d. Jarring of the eggs while turning them.

4th. Too much or not sufficient moisture.

5th. Too much or not sufficient ventilation.

These difficulties may all be easily overcome by the following devices:

HEAT REGULATORS.

I have invented, tested and perfected a Heat Regulator, adapted to any kind of an Incubator having drawers with square corners, of any size, not less than 18x24 inches and not less than $3\frac{1}{4}$ inches deep inside; by means of four flat bars of zinc, one on each side and one on each end, level with the top of the eggs, just outside of the eggs in the drawer. With quadruple compound leverage, the four bars represent an equivalent expansion and contraction of from fourteen hundred to two thousand feet of zinc, which gives an action of from one-fourth to over five-sixteenths of an inch to a degree, and this action is susceptible of being increased or dimin-

3

ished, as desired, in attaching the connecting rod to the valve.

The heated air is drawn from under the heater by means of one or more tin tubes running from below the edge of the bottom of the heater between the heater and egg drawer, outside of the heater on the top, near the center into a valve cup.

The valve cap is placed on the valve cup. When the valve is open the heated air passes through these tubes and out through the valve. The lower ends of these tubes should not extend far enough inward to strike the drawer. When the drawers run close to the heater, holes should be bored through the upper edge of the drawer to allow the heat to pass into the tubes. The valve is connected to the regulator, by rods running outside of the Incubator to the front of the drawer and through the front of the drawer to the regulator.

When the drawer is to be pulled out one rod is unhooked. When the heat rises above the degree, or a fraction of a degree, on which it may be set, the valve will open from $\frac{1}{8}$ to $\frac{3}{4}$ of an inch to a degree, as desired. When the temperature falls to the degree to which it may be set, the valve will close. This will ventilate the eggs and keep the air in a good, healthy condition, and the temperature equal. The degree of heat on the top of the eggs in the drawer is registered on the outside on the top of the Incubator by means of a hand and dial. The regulator may be attached to lamp to turn wick up or down. This is not advisable except for brooders. It is much better to regulate the flame by hand. Should the heat run too high the valve will open in proportion to the intensity of the heat, and let the heat pass out. You should become accustomed to the size the flame should be for your Incubator and burn the wick to supply a little more heat than may be required for 102, 103, or 104 degrees so the valve will open about $\frac{1}{8}$ of an inch (more or less) every one or two hours, and within two hours after the drawer has been pulled out.

The Regulators are as sensitive as any Incubator thermometer. No battery or rubber used; can be easily attached, and are not liable to get out of order. They will require space of two eggs only. Every regulator will be guaranteed to do the work as represented, if attached according to directions, which any one having ordinary mechanical judgment can easily attach and adjust. Price of Regulator complete with cap and valve, for valve cup without the tin tubes, $5.50. Boxing 25 cents.

I find my prices on Regulators will not justify me in furnishing the box, therefore do not waste stamps in writing for discounts.

Instructions sent with each Regulator. In ordering, send the exact inside measurement of the drawer, and state whether it slides in the long way or the short way; also give the exact measurement from the inside of the drawer to the outside front of the Incubator, and state its capacity.

I am not an experimental inventor. Before I undertake to build a new machine it must be complete in my mind in all its parts and in harmony with all the laws governing its actions, otherwise, as a rule, I will not undertake to build the machine. As simple as my Regulators may appear to be they required more experimenting to make them absolutely practical and reliable than all the machines I ever invented. I do not hesitate to state this Regulator is the most practical, reliable and durable Incubator heat Regulator in use.

EGG TURNERS.

My Temperature Divider and Egg Turner combined, has proven a success beyond my expectations. With it an Incubator will hold more eggs than with a slat-turner, of which you will hatch a larger per cent.; the chick will come out much stronger and healthier, from the fact it covers almost the entire surface of the egg-drawer and therefore keeps the eggs cooler on the under side and aids in keeping the heat at a more even temperature on the top, and yet leaves sufficient space for cool air to pass upward for the chicks and for circulation, and does away with the sudden jar which is so injurious to the eggs. It also furnishes a good surface for chicks while hatching. Remember, their position lying across the small slats in their weak condition as they emerge from the shell frequently destroys life. It also, to a great extent, protects the cloth underneath from becoming soiled, and is easily removed to clean the drawer. Iron rods are connected to the Turner so the eggs may be turned without pulling out the drawer. It will pay any one in less than one season to take out their slat-turners and use mine. I guarantee these Turners to do the work and give satisfaction as represented. The advantages of this improvement are too easily comprehended to be mistaken for a frivolous affair. The Turners are light and made in sections, so they can be sent by express at a small cost. Price, complete to fit any drawer 30x42½ or less, $2.50 each. In ordering, send the exact inside measurement of your drawer and the number of inches from the inside of drawer to front of Incubator. State if the drawer slides in the longest or shortest way. I will send full instructions. The Turners are in two parts, so constructed you can turn all the eggs at once, or one-half without turning the balance.

Anyone running a hot air, common sense, hot water, or any kind of Incubator, cannot afford to be without one.

EGG DRAWERS.

Should you want an Egg Drawer complete, with Regulator and Turner attached, made so the large end of the eggs, will be higher than the small end, (the position the eggs should be in to secure the best hatches,) to fit your Incubator, send the exact outside measurement the drawer should be, and the measurement from the inside of the drawer to the front of the Incubator, and also the height the drawer should be. I will furnish a drawer, as above, to hold any number of eggs from 200 to 300, for $10.50, smaller drawers, capacity, 150 eggs, $10.00; 130 eggs, $9.50.

You can build the Incubator after your own plan. I would state, however, that drawers should not be made too large. A large drawer full of eggs cannot be properly attended to while the chicks are coming out, particularly when the weather is a little cold, without great injury to the chicks. A drawer 30x41, with my Turner, will hold 240 eggs and leave 2½ inches space for turning eggs, and sufficient room for each egg so they will not touch, there being no slats to take up space. One rotten egg touching fertile eggs frequently destroys the life germ. I would, however, prefer a smaller drawer; 25x41 inside of drawer will hold 200 eggs. If you want a larger Incubator, make it to hold two, three, four or six drawers.   One Regulator will do for any number of drawers to eight for one Incubator.

I keep Regulators and Turners in stock for drawers 25x28, 25x32, 25x41, 30x40 and 30x41; can fill orders for irregular sizes within ten days from receipt of order.   Tested Incubator Thermometers, 75 cents each, by mail; brass tubes for moisture supply apparatus, 35 cents each, by mail, safe pressed tin Incubator lamps 75 cents, without chimney.   Moisture gauges, 25 cents each, by mail.

Turners and Regulators cannot be sent by mail. I ship them in light boxes, 4 inches deep, from 14 to 18 inches wide, and from 30 to 44 inches long outside.   A Turner, Regulator and box will weigh from 12 to 18 pounds.   One Turner, one Regulator and one box, $8.00.   Additional Turners in same box, $2.00 each; or, two Turners and one box, $5.00.   Additional Turners in same box, $2.00 each. Otherwise, no discount given.

All orders should be accompanied with Bank draft, P. O. money order, or Express money order.   Do not order a Regulator for an inferior Incubator.   I will fill orders for Egg Turners for inferior Incubators but not for Regulators.   My Egg Turners are of that class they will recommend themselves, at first sight, and should you order a Regulator and not order a Turner, when you see one of the Turners you will regret you did not order one, and save express charges.   My Regulators are different.   While they are the best Incubator heat Regulator ever constructed, and will let the hot air pass out until the heat falls to the required degree, partially on the same principle that an engine will let off steam to keep an equal pressure, yet they will not hatch eggs. They simply regulate the heat in the Incubator which is decidedly important, and saves much care, labor, anxiety and many eggs. Regulators are made to fit drawers and when made to fit a drawer of odd dimensions, it cannot be used in a drawer of different size, therefore, do not order C. O. D., on trial, unless you can satisfy me beyond a doubt that you are not only strictly honorable but that you have a good Incubator and know how to run it. Otherwise it might be returned as worthless property, as it would be difficult to find a customer wanting a Regulator same size. As a rule, I will not send goods C. O. D. I give good references and am responsible for what I state and do. Address all orders to J. W. Hile, Valley Falls, Kan.

References for integrity and financial standing, Hicks, Gephart and Co., bankers, Valley Falls, Kansas, or any business man in our city.

INCUBATORS.

Experience has taught me to believe that a hot-air Incubator, made after the common-sense plan, with late improvements, and provided with my Heat Regulator and Turner, will do as good work as any Incubator in use. The Heater should be made perfectly air-tight except where the heat enters and where the gas passes out; otherwise the gas would permeate the filling, enter the egg drawer and injure the eggs. Also take two thicknesses of heavy wrapping paper, one 8x10 and the other 10x12 inches, place a sheet of tin over the paper, 12x14; fasten the same on the bottom of the Heater inside, directly under where the heat enters the heater. This will give you a far more equal heat.

One or more small tubes from one-eighth to three-sixteenths of an inch in diameter, (according to the capacity of Incubator,) running from near the inside corner of the ventilator box, on top of the sand to outside of ventilator box and through the sawdust, near the lamp pipe and heater, to the top of the In cubator, will keep the ventilator box free from carbonic acid gas. This gas, being heavier than pure air, settles like cold air; it flows on the bottom and can easily be drawn to the hottest points and carried off through these tubes by the suction of heat. The tubes in the ventilator box under the eggs should have a cap about 2½ inches in diameter, soldered to each tube ⅛ inch above the tube; this will spread the cold air and prevent the eggs directly over the tubes from becoming injured by cold draughts. Hot water Incubators, those which require filling two or three times a day, require too much wearisome labor, care and guess-work. You guess you have added a sufficient quantity of hot water; you guess the water was hot enough, and you guess the heat will not run up too high before morning; after 20 days hard guessing if you are good at guess-work and have made no other mistake you can guess you will have a fair hatch, but I guess you will spoil a great many eggs in one season. While I cannot class these Incubators with fraud Incubators it is difficult to draw a line of distinction, yet my Regulators will greatly improve their hatching qualities.

In my judgment, the best way to heat an Incubator is with circulating hot water. This will give you the most uniform heat with the least amount of labor and expense. Hard water should never be used.

PLANS FOR CONSTRUCTING THE IMPROVED HAM-
MONTON INCUBATORS.

given below, fills the requirements of nature, equal
to any Incubator manufactured—*no exceptions*—
and at a comparatively small cost.

We will call the drawer 25x41, a No. 0 drawer.
A one drawer Incubator made for one No. 0 drawer
we will call a No. 0 Incubator. A two drawer Incubator made for two No. 0 drawers, we will call a
No. 2 Incubator. A three drawer Incubator made for
3 No. 0 drawers we will call a No. 3 Incubator, and
so on to 8 drawers, each drawer to hold 200 eggs.
We will call a one drawer Incubator, capacity, 240
eggs, a No. 1 Incubator, drawer 30x41 inches inside, and proceed to build a No. 1 Incubator, es-
timating 1 inch common lumber at $\frac{7}{8}$ of an inch
thick and use the same except as hereafter specified.
Make three trusses with 6 legs each of 2x4 lumber
$62\frac{7}{8}$ inches long and 18 inches high. Separate them
18 inches apart, and nail matched flooring on top,
making the floor $50\frac{1}{4}$ inches wide and $61\frac{1}{4}$ inches long,
leaving the ends of the trussels to project $\frac{7}{8}$ of an
inch. Make ventilator frame 8 inches deep, $32\frac{3}{8}$
wide, and $43\frac{3}{8}$ long, outside measurement; fasten
this box to the floor, (on trussels), leaving an equal
space on all sides $8\frac{7}{8}$ inches wide; dress upper edges
of this box for drawer to slide on. The drawer
should be made 5 inches high, $32\frac{3}{8}$ inches wide and
$43\frac{3}{8}$ inches long with an extension for sawdust.
The drawer should be made of 1 and $\frac{1}{4}$ inch hard
lumber that will dress 1 and 3-16ths of an inch thick.
(poplar will do). This will leave your drawer 30x41
inside and will fit ventilator box. The end boards
of the drawer should be $30\frac{3}{8}$ inches long, so you

can set each end in the side board 3-16ths of an inch. Draw a straight pencil mark lengthwise of the end board, $\frac{3}{4}$ of an inch above the lower edge on the inside. Commence 3 inches from each end of each end board and divide the spaces 2 and 7-16ths of an inch apart on the pencil mark, making 11 marks, and bore 11 holes as marked in each end board, $\frac{7}{8}$ of an inch in size, $\frac{1}{4}$ of an inch deep for slats. To make the drawer after the most improved plan so the large end of the eggs will be higher than the small end, to secure the best results, you will want six slats $\frac{7}{8}$x1 inch and 5 slats $\frac{7}{8}$x1$\frac{1}{4}$ inches each 41$\frac{1}{2}$ inches long and two slats for the sides of the drawer 41 inches long and 1 and $\frac{1}{4}$ inches wide and $\frac{3}{4}$ of an inch thick. Plane the upper corners of the thick slats so they will not be over $\frac{1}{2}$ inch wide on the top. Place one, 1 inch slat between each 1 and $\frac{1}{4}$ inch slat; cut each end of the 1 and $\frac{1}{4}$ inch slats, so they will project $\frac{1}{4}$ of an inch above the 1 inch slats; the slats should be on a level on the underside and $\frac{1}{4}$ of an inch above the lower edge of the drawer. Each end should be cut to fit the holes and a nail driven through each end board in the ends of the slats. Nail or screw a strip of heavy hoop iron, 30 inches long, crosswise in the center to the under side of the slats. Stretch heavy, coarsely woven muslin over the slats in the drawer, and nail strips of lath $\frac{3}{8}$ of an inch wide and $\frac{1}{4}$ of an inch thick on the top of the cloth to the 1 inch slats to make them level with the 1$\frac{1}{4}$ inch slats. I have given the length of the drawer as 43$\frac{3}{8}$ inches; but remember, this is a mistake on purpose. The side boards of the drawer should be 9$\frac{3}{4}$ inches longer, making the drawer 53$\frac{1}{8}$ inches long, with another end board 1 and 3-16ths inches thick and five inches wide, leaving a space of eight and 9-16ths by thirty inches for sawdust, the same being the front of the drawer, which will come even with the outside of the Incubator, to which you can fasten handles for pulling out the drawers. Next, bore five 9-16th inch holes through the bottom of the floor, in the ventilator box, as follows; one in the center, or as near as possible, to miss the truss underneath, bore the other four 10 inches from each corner towards the center of the box. Insert a tube 7 inches long in each hole, letting them project $\frac{1}{8}$ of an inch below the bottom; tubes to be made of heavy tin 9-16ths outside diameter, solder a small wire on each opposite side of the top of each tube; bend these wires $\frac{1}{2}$ inch above the tubes in opposite directions, and solder to them a cap $2\frac{1}{2}$ inches in diameter. Fill this ventilator box with sand within $\frac{1}{4}$ inch of the top of the ventilator tubes. Place your drawer on your ventilator box, and nail one board 14 inches wide and 32 and 7-16ths inches long firmly to back end of the ventilator box letting the board rest on the floor with planed side next to drawer; nail one board to each side of ventilator box 14 inches in width and 54 inches long; the drawer should project $\frac{7}{8}$ of an inch in front. The upper edges of these boards directly over front end of drawer should be cut down even with the top of the drawer. The board covering this end of the drawer should be $8\frac{7}{8}$ of an inch wide and $34\frac{1}{2}$ long leaving the drawer to project $\frac{7}{8}$ of an inch. Nail a cleat or strip of board to front end of ventilator box $\frac{7}{8}$ of an inch below the edge and one short cleat to the side-boards under the end of the drawer to nail a board under front end of drawer to, where the

space is filled with sawdust. The heater box should
be 6 inches deep inside, $44\frac{1}{4}$ inches long and $34\frac{1}{8}$
inches wide outside. Cover the top with matched
lumber planed side downward. Cover the bottom
with galvanized iron, make it air tight. First arrange the corners where lamp tubes will come, with
tin and paper as described on page 15. Place this
box on the boards nailed to the ventilator box with
galvanized iron downward. Nail one strip of board
to the front end of the heater box to which to nail the
top board, covering the front end of drawer. This
will complete your frame for drawer. Bore holes for
heater tubes through the top of the heater as follows. Should you want the front lamp on the left
hand front corner, bore four $\frac{3}{4}$ inch holes opposite
the lamp within 2 inches of the side-board on the
right hand side commencing within 2 inches of the
end board opposite the lamp, measure from board
to center of hole, and from center of hole to center
of hole, bore 2nd hole $7\frac{1}{2}$ inches from 1st hole, 3rd
hole 8 inches from 2nd, 4th hole $8\frac{1}{2}$ inches from
3rd hole, leaving a space of 18 inches, for lamp tubes
on the back right hand side. Opposite this space
commence near the corner as above, and bore 4 more
holes leaving another space of 18 inches for lamp
tube, on the front left hand corner. These holes
will require 8 heavy tin tubes, 22 inches long and
$\frac{3}{4}$ of an inch in diameter; the tubes should be placed
in these holes perpendicularly, within $\frac{5}{8}$ of an inch
of the galvanized iron. To prevent the galvanized
iron from flopping and putting out the lamps, run
4 or more wires through the heater, place a small
ferrell over the end of each wire, bend wire over ferrell and solder fast; draw upper end tightly, bend

over and fasten with staples on top. The holes for the lamp tubes should be cut in the sides of heater box, the shape of a spectacle eye, $3\frac{1}{2}$x$1\frac{1}{2}$ inches in size. Center of hole should be 4 inches above the galvanized iron in the 18 inch spaces, from center of heater tube to center of lamp tube, $9\frac{1}{2}$ inches, leaving $7\frac{1}{2}$ inches from center of lamp tube to end board. Your lamp elbows should be 7x1$4\frac{3}{4}$ outside. Measurement short end of tube for common lamp chimney should be $3\frac{3}{8}$ of an inch in diameter, opposite end $2\frac{3}{4}$ or 3 inches, press this end together to form shape of a spectacle eye two inches wide. Cut hole through heavy tin same shape to fit over end of tube. Before nailing this tin to the heater you should arrange the hot air moisture apparatus, this, however, is not particularly necessary as there are other means by which you can supply moisture just as well. It is simply a matter of convenience and economy, it requires no egg space.

HOT AIR MOISTURE APPARATUS.

For this apparatus you will require a brass tube, 20 inches long, from $\frac{1}{8}$ to 3-16ths of an inch in diameter, letting the tube project 4 inches in the heater; run a tin tube 4 inches long from this end, down through the galvanized iron $\frac{1}{8}$ below the iron, solder tube to the iron; from this end run another tube diagonally across the bottom of the heater on opposite side near opposite lamp outside and downward in a cup of water. The cup of water is simply to prevent the cold air from passing upward in the heater. The tube under the heater should be soldered close to the heater and run on a slight incline, so the steam which may condense in the tube will be carried off in the cup. The tube should be split open on the upper side near the center of the heater to allow the steam or moisture to pass out; this tube may be from $\frac{1}{4}$ to $\frac{3}{8}$ of an inch in diameter. Next bore a hole in the end of the elbow within $\frac{1}{4}$ inch or less of the top, to let the brass tube pass through. Lamp tubes should be incased in a box 10 inches square and 18 inches long; cut a hole through the lower side of the box, near the end, $4\frac{1}{4}$ inches in diameter for lamp tube; insert a 2 ℔ fruit can in this hole. Cut a hole through the lower end of can to fit lamp tube. Top of can should be left open and the edge bent over to hold it in place. Let the lamp pipe come just below the can, and fill box and can around the pipe with sand or clay. After your lamp attachments and box, covering lamp tubes, are completed, all but filling and nailing on end and top board of lamp tube box, take a heavy piece of galvanized iron 3 inches square, bore a hole through the center, place a stopcock in the hole and solder firmly; run tube from the lower end of stop-cock to outer end of brass tube; run another tube from upper end of stopcock to the bottom edge of a 2 quart can on top of lamp tube box. You can regulate this to supply any degree of moisture. A No. 1 Incubator will require 2 carbonic acid gas tubes a trifle over $\frac{1}{8}$ of an inch in diameter; about $\frac{1}{8}$ of an inch area to 100 eggs, is sufficient; the suction is strong and constant and the Regulator will aid.

These tin tubes can be easily made by running tin over wire, and pulling out the wire and soldering.

A No. 1 Incubator Heat Regulator will require one tin tube 1 and $\frac{5}{8}$ of an inch in diameter opposite each lamp. Area of these tubes should be about

1 and $\frac{1}{2}$ inches to 100 eggs. Attach as described on page 4. These tubes should be made larger where they enter the egg chamber and pressed together, so they will not be over one inch wide and close to the heater. Board up outside of Incubator 14 inches above the top of heated box, fill and pack with sawdust and cover with lumber. You should have trusses, or some substantial arrangement on a level with the bottom of your egg-drawers outside of Incubator, to rest your drawers on.

A one drawer Incubator made for a No. 0 drawer should be made in every way just the same as a No. 1 Incubator except there should be 4 ventilator tubes in the ventilator box instead of 5 and they should be placed 3 inches nearer the center. This Incubator will be 5 inches narrower inside and outside than the No. 1 and will hold 200 eggs.

A No. 2 Incubator is made by placing two No. 0 drawers together. Ventilator box should be $54\frac{3}{4}$x-$43\frac{3}{8}$ inches outside measurement, with 4 ventilator tubes under each drawer, same as No. 0 Incubator.

Place a 2x8 in the center for drawers to slide on. Bore five or six holes through the 2x8 for air to circulate through above the sand. The heater box should be $56\frac{1}{2}$x$44\frac{1}{4}$ inches outside. Arrange 3 lamp tubes same as in No. 1 Incubator. Place them on the back of the Incubator one in the center, and one the same distance from each corner as in No. 1 Incubator. Place one $\frac{5}{8}$ inch tube in the heater box within 1 inch of the side board in the center between each end of lamp tube and one tube on the right, and one on the left hand side of Incubator, within one inch of the side and within 8 inches of each front corner. Place seven $\frac{3}{4}$ inch tubes in front

within one inch of front side 8 and $\frac{1}{2}$ inches apart.
The corner tubes will come within 1 and $\frac{1}{2}$ inches
of the corners. This Incubator will require 1 piece
of 2x6 lumber, well nailed to the front of the heater
to support the weight of the packing with a brace
under each end of the 2x6.   A No. 3 hot air Incubator is made just the same as a No. 2 Incubator,
except place 3 No. 0 drawers side by side with two
2x8 for drawers to slide on.   Ventilator box will be
$82\frac{1}{8}$x$43\frac{3}{8}$ inches; heater box will be $83\frac{7}{8}$x$44\frac{1}{4}$ inches.

This Incubator will require two $\frac{5}{8}$ inch tubes between each lamp ten tubes in front and one on each
right and left hand side.   Use 2x8 instead of a 2x6
to support the packing.   A No. 3 will require a
very little larger lamp flame than a No. 2.

A No. 4 Incubator is made by placing four No.
0 drawers together, two side by side and end to end.
Drawers pull out in opposite directions.   The ven-
tilator box should be 54 and $\frac{3}{4}$ by 86 and $\frac{3}{4}$ inches.
A 2x8 should be placed in the center of this box
for drawers to slide on, with holes bored for air to
circulate through.   This Incubator will require 4
lamps two on each side, same distance from each
corner, as No. 1 Incubator, and 16 heater tubes $\frac{5}{8}$ of
an inch in diameter, 24 inches long, and six $\frac{3}{4}$ inch
heater tubes 24 inches long.

Place two $\frac{3}{4}$ inch tubes on each side that the
lamps are on, within 4 inches of the center on the
side. (8 inches apart.)   Place two $\frac{5}{8}$ inch tubes between each $\frac{3}{4}$ inch tube and each lamp.   Place
one $\frac{3}{4}$ inch tube in the center in each front side
of heater box and each corner.   This Incubator
should have 16 inches of sawdust on the top, and
will require four 2x8 nailed to the top of the heater.

For a 150 egg Incubator make your drawer 25x32 inches. Ventilator box should be $27\frac{3}{8}$ by $24\frac{3}{8}$. Heater box $29\frac{1}{8}$ by $34\frac{1}{8}$ outside. This Incubator will require six $\frac{3}{4}$ inch heater tubes, three opposite each lamp. Otherwise make it the same as No. 1 except bore four $\frac{1}{2}$ inch holes, for ventilator tubes instead of four 5-16th inch holes.

A 130 egg drawer should be 25x28 inches inside measurement. Ventilator box should be $27\frac{3}{4}$ by $32\frac{3}{8}$. Heater box $29\frac{1}{8}$ by $33\frac{1}{4}$ outside. This will require one lamp in the back, or on one side in the center, and one $\frac{5}{8}$ inch heater tube in each corner of the heater box and two $\frac{5}{8}$ tubes opposite the lamp 8 inches apart. Four tubes are sufficient for ventilator box.

The 150 and 130 egg drawers will make good sizes for double Incubators.

Remember the ventilator boxes are all made 8 inches deep, the floors should extend on all sides of ventilator boxes, $8\frac{7}{8}$ inches, before the 14 inch boards are nailed to the ventilator. The heater boxes are all made six inches deep, and rest on the top edge of the 14 inch boards, one inch above the egg drawer. The 14 inch boards upon which the heater box rests should be screwed to one or two 2x4 pieces of lumber and a wedge placed between the 2x4 and the heater box, to prevent the packing from tightening the drawer.

HOT WATER INCUBATOR.

The most practical, economical hot water Incubator which can be made, at the least cost, can be made as follows. For a No. 0, a No. 1, or a 150 egg drawer make the Incubator in every way, as a hot air Incubator except the heater box which should be 10 inches deep instead of 6 inches, make a galvanized iron tank to fit inside of box. Nail upper edge well to box and solder over nail heads. Matched lumber will do for cover but galvanized iron soldered on, is better. Make long end of your lamp pipe 17 inches long, 2½ inches in diameter, place an elbow on the front left hand lamp tube and run a 2½ inch pipe back within 5 or 6 inches of the inside of the tank, place another elbow on this tube and run it to the center of the tank on back end, place another elbow on this end and run pipe to the center of the tank into an upright pipe 2½ inches in diameter, 20 inches long. Arrange pipe for right hand lamp same way on opposite side and run in same upright pipe. These pipes should be well soldered to prevent their leaking. Strips of tin should be soldered over the pipe and to the galvanized iron on the bottom to prevent them from raising when the tank is filled. These pipes should run within about 3 inches of the sides and ends and be about 3½ inches above the bottom of the tank. There should be a damper in the upper end of upright pipe to regulate draught. The damper should work hard so it will stay where it may be placed. Make the 130 egg Incubator the same, except run the pipes from corner to corner, 3 inches from the sides and to near where you started into upright pipe 2½ inches in diameter. This pipe should be made of heavy tin or galvanized iron. The only parts of the Poultry Keeper and Farm and Garden Incubator, you will require for these Incubators will be a funnel and a water-cock, to pour in and draw off water when necessary. Fill tank with hot water to start with. These tanks will require to be well supported with three rows of heavy wire or small bolts running through the tank and up through 2x4 pieces of lumber with brace under each end to support the weight. These wires or bolts should be well soldered on the bottom. Two rows of wire or bolts will do for the small Incubators, 14 inches of sawdust are sufficient on the tank. You can fasten small shelves, to your Incubator under the lamp tubes; place a small box under the lamp. To take the lamp out, remove the box, or nail a small board to the edge of a board 8 inches wide and fasten it to the Incubator with hinges to swing out of the way to take out lamp in which case you will require a hook and staple to hold it in position, otherwise the lamp would not be safe fixed in this way. I do not manufacture or solicit orders for Incubators, yet we have good mechanics in our city who understand building them and I can have them made so a one drawer Incubator with lamps, one moisture gauge, 1 thermometer, and complete in every particular, except filling with sand and sawdust, delivered on the cars in Valley Falls, will not cost to exceed from $25 to $40 each, according to size, style and finish, $2.00 less without moisture supply apparatus. Labor and lumber may be cheaper in your locality, in which case you could have them built cheaper than I could, and save the freight.

In filling orders for Incubators I will allow six inches space for sawdust on the sides and 12 inches on the top, unless otherwise ordered.

A sudden change of temperature will not affect these Incubators. It is not necessary to place them in the cellar, any building will do, so the wind does not blow through sufficient to affect the lamp flame. The Incubators should be at least 18 inches above the floor or ground.

WALLS OF INCUBATORS.

The Incubators as described may appear somewhat bulky, yet for a cheaply constructed building in a climate where the changes of temperature are great, the walls are not too thick, otherwise four inches of saw dust would be sufficient for the sides which would make the Incubators 8 inches shorter 8 inches narrower, and the lamp pipes 4 inches shorter. To guard against fire, short lamp tube will require a strip of tin in the heater directly over end of lamp tubes. As heat has a tendency to rise and pass through, you should have at least from 8 to 12 inches of sawdust on the top. For a light Incubator for a room, or a climate, where the changes of temperature are not very great, make a box 8 inches deep same size of your heater box, nail it to the top of the heater, give this inside tier of boxes a thin coating of coal tar and resin on the outside to exclude air; nail strips of board $\frac{7}{8}$ of an inch square around the top on the outside of the box on the heater. Nail strips same size perpendicularly 21 inches long, 12 or 14 inches apart under first strips, and tack building paper to the strips, nail strips same size on top of the paper to first strips, and stretch building paper over the strips and nail $\frac{1}{2}$ inch lumber on the outside. This will give you a double air space. Fill upper box with sawdust and cover with $\frac{1}{2}$ inch lumber. By making ventilator box 2 inches narrower, a 120 egg Incubator made in this way would be $33\frac{1}{4}$ by $36\frac{1}{4}$ inches and $21\frac{3}{8}$ inches outside measurement, which is as small as an Incubator of same capacity should be made. The secret of success is not in the thickness of the walls or how they should be constructed; but in the general provisions for supplying the requirements of nature. The walls should be made to counteract the outside changes of temperature.

CIRCULATING HOT WATER INCUBATORS.

These are heated with hot water, running through small boilers connected to one inch gas or steam pipe. No tin lamp tubes, galvanized iron or tin heater tubes required. The heaters are left open on the bottom. The boilers should be round, $7\frac{1}{2}$ inches in diameter on the bottom (with copper bottom) and $1\frac{1}{2}$ to 2 inches on top and 8 inches high. For Incubator of less than 6 drawers, one boiler is sufficient, and the pipe should run as follows. Place an elbow on one end of the pipe and solder elbow in the top of the boiler, run the pipe from the boiler in the heater box within two inches of the side, to within 2 inches of the opposite side or end, from the boiler and back and forth in the heater from $2\frac{1}{4}$ to $2\frac{1}{2}$ inches apart and back and out to the lower edge of the boiler.

The pipe should be on a gradual incline of 3 inches from the top of the pipe where it enters the heater box to where it passes out of the heater box. Heater box should be 6 inches deep. The pipe should enter the box within two inches of the top and come out within one inch of the lower edge of the heater and should be suspended in the heater with hooks or wire. Bend the lower end of the pipe (outside of the heater) downward to reach the lower edge of the boiler. Supply tank should be from 8 to 12 inches square and 5 or 6 inches deep. The bottom of the supply tank should be on a level with the top end of the steam pipe.

Run a tube $\frac{1}{8}$ of an inch in diameter from the bottom of the supply tank to the bottom edge of the boiler. Run another tube same size from the top of the elbow (on top of the boiler) 2 inches above the supply tank. Bend the tube downward, 4 inches below supply tank, bend upwards and solder the tube in the bottom of the supply tank. This will act as a blow off and keep the water warm, in the tank and aid in circulating the water. Keep the tank covered. Hard water should not be used. The boilers are heated with gasoline and gasoline stove burners. Coal oil will not do, as it would soon form a coating of soot on the bottom of the boiler. Soot being a strong non-conductor of heat, the heat would soon run down in the Incubator.

The steam pipes running from the Incubator to the boiler should be covered with tin tubes about one inch larger than the pipes, the boiler should also have an outside covering or casing about one inch larger every way than the boiler, and should project not less than one-half inch below the edge of the boiler. This casing will keep the cold air from coming in direct contact with the boiler and pipe.

A No. 6 Incubator is made by placing 6 No. 0 drawers together, 3 side by side and 3 end to end. Ventilator box should be $82\frac{1}{8}$ by $130\frac{1}{8}$ inches outside. Heater box $83\frac{7}{8}$ by $130\frac{1}{8}$ inches.

A No. 8 Incubator is made by placing 4 No. 0 drawers side by side and 4 end to end.

Ventilator box should be $110\frac{3}{8}$ by $130\frac{1}{8}$ inches outside. The center 2 by 8 for drawers to slide on should have a strip $\frac{7}{8}$ of an inch thick nailed to it to make it thicker on the top and a strip $\frac{7}{8}$ of an inch square nailed on the top to separate the middle drawers, so an upright brace may be placed between the front end of the center drawers to support the weight of packing.

A No. 6 and a No. 8 Incubator should have two boilers, which should be on a level and the pipes arranged, with every other turn $9\frac{1}{2}$ inches apart and $2\frac{1}{4}$ or $2\frac{1}{2}$ inches apart so that one turn will fit in the other and be about $2\frac{1}{4}$ or $2\frac{1}{2}$ inches apart. When put together the pipe should run from the top of one boiler into the lower end of the opposite boiler, and by placing the pipes on an incline, as above described it will place one half of the pipe, above the other half each side from the center in the heater. The heater for No's. 6 and 8 should also be nailed to 2 by 6 lumber to support the weight of packing.

These Incubators are made the same as the hot air Incubators, except as stated on pages 23, 24.

So many have written me (without enclosing stamps) to know if my Incubators would work without my attachments. If you will add the carbonic acid gas tubes and the caps over ventilator tubes, there is not an Incubator made that will do any better work without a heat Regulator and Egg Turner than those described in this book. Without my Turner the bottom of the drawer should be level. I consider all Incubators comparatively frauds, without a heat Regulator and some way by which to turn the eggs otherwise than by hand.

CIRCULATING HOT WATER MOISTURE APPARATUS.

Run a half inch pipe from the top of the boiler or steam pipe, through the heater above the inside pipe, to outside and down in a cup of water. Place a stop-cock in this pipe near the boiler to regulate the moisture.

There should be a number of small holes bored in the upper side of the pipe to let the steam pass out in the heater. A hand hole in the heater so you can place pans of water on the top of the steam pipe will do as well.

RULES FOR RUNNING AN INCUBATOR.

Do not cool your eggs too much. If you pull out your drawers twice a day, from two to ten minutes is sufficient for cooling, according to the outside temperature.

If your Incubator is provided with one of my heat Regulators, when it is thoroughly adjusted, and when the dial is marked to indicate the degrees of temperature on the top of the eggs, and you know there is sufficient moisture, it is not necessary to pull out the drawer more than once or twice a week.

With Regulator, and Turner, pulling out the drawer to cool the eggs is unnecessary. I sometimes let my Incubator run 10 days without pulling out the drawer except to test the eggs, and have hatched as high as 94 per cent. of fertile eggs. I consider 75 per cent. a small hatch if the eggs are No. 1.

Before you fill your Incubator run it 2 or 3 days or until you thoroughly understand it, and get the rods properly adjusted. The heat should be about 108 degrees in the Incubator when you fill it, the eggs will cool it down. Up to the 14th day of incubation hold the heat as near 103 degrees as possible then reduce the heat to 102 degrees, in warm weather.

In cold weather it is better to hold the heat at 104 degrees the first 14 days, then drop to 103 degrees, as in cold weather it requires more heat to have the right degree of heat below the centre of the eggs. As the warm weather advances, you can reduce the heat, but not below 102 degrees even after the 14th day. Turn the eggs twice a day at least, three times would be better. The practice of rolling the eggs by hand, is a very bad one, for three reasons. First, in cold weather it takes too long. Second, you jar them more or less by knocking them together. 3d, the per cent. lost by hand handling will not pay. The turn-over trays are very little better. It is much better to roll the eggs over by one motion without jarring them.

Never sprinkle your eggs. Too much moisture, particularly in the first stages of incubation, causes the chick to grow so rapidly it fills the shell so tightly, that when it is ready to come out, it cannot turn in the shell to pick its way out, and therefore pierces the shell with its bill and dies.

If your Incubator is not provided with my apparatus for supplying moisture, zinc pans of water under the egg drawer will answer the purpose. In using pans, ordinarly 64 square inches of surface to 100 eggs is sufficient, or in that proportion, according to the capacity of your Incubator. Yet, during rainy or damp weather, or in localities where the atmosphere is very damp, less would be better. In high altitudes where the atmosphere is very dry, 64 inches would not be sufficient. Make your pans to hold about 50 square inches to 100 eggs, then add and take out smaller vessels to suit the conditions of atmosphere and the different stages of incubation.

In cold weather the eggs will require more water surface under the egg drawer than in warm weather.

The sand and.saw-dust, or filling in the incubator, should be dry to commence with, otherwise you might have too much moisture. The safest way would be to use a moisture guage.   My improved guages will give you the proper degree of humidity necessary to produce best results.   In any climate, longitude, latitude or altitude where man can work, breathe and live, chicks can be hatched.   Sufficient water surface should be supplied so the guage will fall from $2\frac{1}{2}$ to 3 degrees in 24 hours, up to the 5th or 6th day of incubation, then add more water surface, so the guage will fall 2 degrees in 24 hours.

The 17th or 18th day of incubation increase the moisture so the guage will fall about $1\frac{1}{2}$ degrees in 24 hours.   This may be done by placing cups of wet sand in the egg drawer, (cloth or sponges in cups will sour, smell badly and permeate the air) or by spraying the eggs slightly, once or twice a day. Better to add more water surface under the drawer. When the eggs are cooled to 90 degrees or less, with experience you can readily pick out the unfertile and dead eggs by feeling them; they will be colder than the fertile eggs.   When eggs begin to ooze or sweat, take them out they will injure the eggs near them. You will gain more by filling the space left by taking out the unsound eggs than by leaving it vacant.   The loss from the slight variations of heat and moisture the added eggs will be subjected to, will be slight.

Never add cold eggs to warm eggs in an incubation.   It would be better to place a cloth in a box, place your eggs in the box and cover with two or three thicknesses of cloth.   Place a thermometer in the box on the top of the cloth; place the same in your cooking stove oven; leave the doors partially open, and keep the thermometer on the top at from 100 to 103 degrees from 2 to 3 hours, or until the thermometer under the cloth rises to 98 degrees. It is better to fill your drawer at the commencement.

If your Incubator holds two or more drawers, you can safely fill one every day or two after filling first drawer, by warming the eggs as above. Regardless of the capacity of your Incubator, it should be furnished with at least three correct thermometers. If your Incubator will distribute the heat uniformly, which it should do, the thermometers may be placed side by side, but resting against different eggs; the top of the bulb should be even with the top of the eggs, opposite end of the thermometer should be a very little higher than the bulb; place one or two small blocks of wood under each thermometer to raise them. If the thermometers register alike from 102 to 103 degrees, but not over 104 degrees, you may expect all is well. But if they vary from 1 to 3 degrees, something is wrong, probably one thermometer may rest on a fertile egg and one on an unfertile egg and one on a rotten egg; or, if the chicks are about ready to come out, a chick may have struggled in the shell and worked up a fever heat and raised the mercury. No matter, you should find the difficulty before changing the temperature, this you can do by testing the three eggs. Always keep the bulb of the thermometer against fertile eggs. Do not burn your lamp flame too high, or you will ventilate your eggs too much. If the valve cap opens slightly now and then, it is sufficient. when you remove the lamp to fill and trim, always place a cloth or something in the lamp tube to prevent the strong draught of air from cooling the heater.

Never press or pull the turner rods with a jerk·
Should an egg get broken in the Incubator and stick
to the turner, open the drawer and raise the turner
carefully to loosen it. Slide the drawer in and out
carefully; use black lead to make it slide easily.
Never use grease. 108 or even 110 degrees will do
little damage for a few hours. When overheated pull
out the drawer and let the eggs cool down to 80 or 85
degrees.

When hatching in cold weather tack a piece of
cardboard under the Incubator over each ventilator
hole, to cover about one-half of each hole. When
you open the drawer while the chicks are hatching,
remove the loose shells quickly and guard against
keeping the drawer out too long or you may chill
and injure the chicks before they are dry; do not
remove them until they are dry, then place them in
warm quarters. The above rules will apply to almost any Incubator in use.

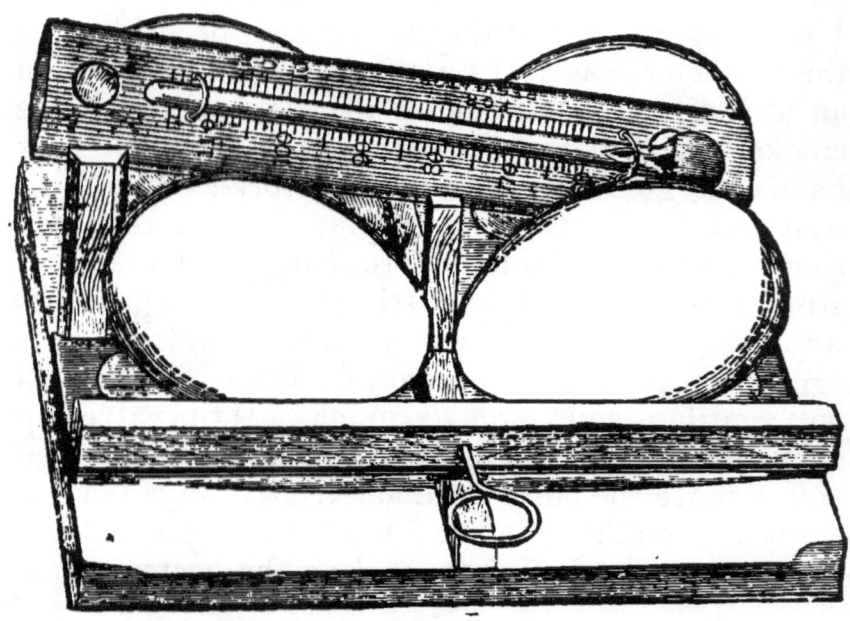

This cut represents the bottom of the egg drawer and egg turner with rod for turning the eggs; also 4 eggs with thermometer in position.
These thermometers are made to order by

JOHN KENDALL & CO.,

NEW LEBANON, N. Y.,

Manufacturers of

Thermometers for Incubators, Dairy House Window Show, Registering, Decorative Art and Fancy Work. Also Aneroid Barometers, Hydromters, &c., &c.

Goods made to Order in any Style or Quality.

Send for Catalogue.

I furnish the Incubator Thermometers with blocks for 75 cents by mail.

INCUBATION.

Ill-shaped eggs or unnatural sizes are not profitable to incubate. Insufficient heat will retard incubation, produce weakly chicks, and not unfrequently prevent the chicks from properly absorbing the yelks and from healing as they otherwise would.

Too much heat and moisture will force an unnatural growth, and produce deformity and weakness.

When the large ends of the eggs are higher than the smaller ends, the chicks invariably form with their heads in the large ends, and can pick their way out more easily. And should their bill be downward when they take their first breath, they are not apt to drown by the water and mucous in the shell. When the small ends of the eggs are higher than the large ends (during the first stages of incubation,) the chicks are apt to form with their heads in the smaller ends, many of which cannot pick their way out. My Incubator drawers and turners are arranged to obviate these difficulties. These turners will work just as well on a level surface as on an irregular surface. The only object in having the bottom of the drawer irregular, is, the turners will keep the eggs in proper position for hatching, which is more important than is generally supposed; thousands of chicks drown in their shells.

My drawers and turners prevent this difficulty; with them you will hatch a larger per cent. of eggs. The turners are also temperature dividers, as well as egg turners; they divide the upper stratum of air from the lower, and therefore keep the eggs cooler on the under side, which aids in producing a healthier circulation of blood. When the eggs are turned, warm side downward, the little veins contract, and force the blood upwards, then follows a reaction, and the blood rushes to the lower side to aid in supplying warmth.

This also proves one of the necessities of turning the eggs, the turners make the necessary difference in the temperature between the upper and lower part of the egg to produce a healthier circulation of the blood while the chick is being formed, and therefore produces a stronger, healthier chick. A larger per cent. of eggs can be hatched and the chicks will be stronger and healthier hatched with proper artificial means than with hens, but not with fraud Incubators.

Many Incubators are entirely too small in proportion to the number of eggs they are intended to hold. In crowding so many eggs into a small space, you lose many by the accumulation of carbonic acid gas, and deprive the eggs and chicks of pure oxygen, which is necessary to sustain life. If you could keep a proper degree of humidity and temperature, it would be difficult to injure the eggs by giving them too much space and draught. The philoso. phy is, the heat dries the air, the draught carries off the moisture, and too much draught will carry off the moisture faster than the water will evaporate sufficiently to keep the eggs in good condition, therefore the chicks will dry in the shell and die.

Strong, healthy chicks are not altogether due, however, to the best mode of hatching, but, to a great extent, to the age, vigor, and health of the parents. Then, again, to produce best results, birds should be supplied with proper food, in sufficient quantities, so the eggs will be supplied with such fluids in sufficient quantities necessary to produce best results. Their natural appetite will dictate to them such varieties of food as they may require from time to time to supply deficiencies, if the same may be within their reach. A hen has no knowledge of science, should she succeed in hatching every egg, it would be due to strict attention to business, under favorable circumstances.

EGG TESTER.

One of the best. Make a tight box 10 inches square outside; paint it black inside. Make a hole 3 inches in diameter, in one end, stretch and tack a piece of soft leather over the hole, cut a hole in the leather 1 inch wide and 1½ inches long the shape of an egg Bore an inch hole in the center of the opposite end, and place a tube in this hole, 6 inches long, letting it project 5 inches. This tube may be tin or paper. Place the box so the large end of the egg

will be upward, and from you; cut another hole in
the center of the box on the right hand side, large
enough to pass your hand in with an egg. Place a
black cloth over the box to cover your hand to exclude the light. Press the egg lightly against the
heater on the inside, large end up and look through
to a bright lamp-light—sunlight is better. I usu-
ally test my eggs the sixth or seventh day of Incubation, and take out all unfertile eggs. You can
see a dark spot floating in the upper part of a fertile
egg; from this spot you can see small veins running in various directions. Unfertile eggs will have
the appearance of a fresh egg and
should be left out.

STANDARD MOISTURE GAUGE.

I am indebted to J. L. Camp-
bell, the famous Eureka Incubator man, of West Elizabeth, Pa.,
through the *Poultry Keeper*, for
the idea of this gauge. His gauge
is a straight glass tube, $\frac{3}{4}$ of an
inch in diameter, from four to six
inches long, set in a block of wood.

My gauges are 3 inches high,
upper part $\frac{1}{2}$ inch in diameter,
lower part 1 and 5-16 inches. The
degree marks are closer together
than as represented in the cut.
The gauges are filled with water
and placed in the egg drawer.
The moisture is supplied by placing pans of water under the egg
drawer, or with cups of wet sand
in the drawer or with moisture ap-

paratus. If you have sufficient moisture in your Incubator so the water in the gauge will evaporate as described on page 28, the moisture will be just right. Should the water evaporate faster in the gauge, add more moisture. Should it not evaporate fast enough in the gauge, diminish the supply of moisture. You will find these gauges absolutely reliable. They should be filled every two or three days, until the moisture supply is adjusted to the right degree. Price of these gauges is 25 cents, by mail. Length, $2\frac{3}{8}$, $2\frac{5}{8}$ and 3 inches. Will send 3 inch gauges unless otherwise ordered.

BROODERS.

The following Brooders are made two stories high, each story is divided in two parts. You should have two Brooders for each one drawer Incubator. The chicks should be placed in the upper story until they are three weeks old, then placed below to give room for the next brood.

For one Brooder make two heaters, one six inches deep and one four inches deep, 28x48 inches outside. Cover one side of each box with galvanized iron, and nail matched lumber to the edges of the six inch box over the iron. Place a few small screws through the iron in the matched lumber to keep the iron from sagging. Cut holes in one side of the six inch box for the lamp, same as for No.2 Incubator. Next, place the four inch box (with galvanized iron downward) on top of the six inch box, and bore seven $\frac{3}{4}$ of an inch holes near the side opposite where the lamp will come, through the iron and matched boards, about eight inches apart; bore two more holes within four inches of the center on the side on which the lamps are placed. Bore a $\frac{7}{4}$ of an inch hole in the center for ventilator tube. Make a box twelve inches deep, 28x48 inside to fit outside of the four inch box; let this box project $1\frac{1}{2}$ inches below the galvanized iron, and nail to heater. Make another box eight inches deep, same size, to fit over lower heater; let this box project 2 inches below the heater and nail to the heater. Separate these boxes, so the lower edge of upper outside box will come $3\frac{1}{2}$ inches above the top of the lower heater; nail three strips two inches wide on each side of these boxes, letting the ends project $3\frac{3}{4}$ inches below the lower edge of the heater for legs. Next, place nine 12 inch heater tubes in the holes, letting them come within $\frac{3}{4}$ of an inch of the lower galvanized iron (when nailed on), solder these tubes to the iron to prevent them from leaking gas.

Place one $\frac{7}{8}$ inch tube 30 inches long in the center within $\frac{3}{4}$ of an inch of the lower floor, place another $\frac{7}{8}$ inch tube $13\frac{5}{8}$ inches long by the side of this long tube in the upper heater, let it come within $\frac{3}{4}$ of an inch of the upper floor and solder these tubes to the iron. Arrange a sheet of zinc 12 inches square, with paper underneath, in the heater above, and below the end of lamp tubes where the heat enters, and nail galvanized iron on the bottom 28x48 inches, letting the outside box project below the iron. Cover top of inside box with matched lumber and fill with sawdust. Lamp tubes should be boxed the same as for an Incubator. Long end of tubes should be 2 inches shorter. To divide the Brooders in two divisions saw in the 8 and 12 inch boards on each side in the center up to the iron and stretch through a strip of wire netting, tack cotton flannel to the 8 and 12 inch boards to rest on the chicks. Each division of each Brooder should have heavy building paper well oiled to slide in on each floor, to be taken out and cleaned while the chicks are outside. The slides should be drawn out from each end. The heater tubes should be protected with wire netting to keep the chicks from being pressed against them and injured by heat. There should be a heavy fringe tacked around upper and lower division to reach the floor; each floor should be 6 inches wide on all sides. Make the runways for lower divisions of Brooder on each end; runways for upper divisions should be on the side opposite the lamps. A cheaply constructed building 12x16 will do for two double Brooders and will accommodate 440 chicks and leave an alley way through the center to attend to lamps, &c. The chicks should have larger runways outside of the buildings.

FEEDING AND CARE OF LITTLE CHICKS.

No doubt the following will meet with opposition as nearly all have their own ideas on the subject. The word is, feed unfertile, hard boiled eggs. I have had enough experience in that direction and decline to agree with public opinion on that point. Fertile or unfertile eggs, eggs that are not stale are excellent food for young chicks; also for hens; but not hard boiled. It is not their natural food as represented. Hard boiled yelks are not easily digested, they also cause constipation. Chicks should be fed within from 18 to 24 hours after they are hatched. Bread crumbs moistened with raw egg, and boiled wheat is excellent. After they are 3 days old give them all the dry grain they will eat. Wheat, cracked corn, millet, sorghum seed, etc. etc., as follows: Their first feed in the morning should be boiled

wheat or soft food: add a little finely chopped cook-
ed meat or egg, to their soft food, and about one-
half as much salt as you would use to salt food for
the table.   Give them as much as they will eat up
clean, and no more.   During the day let them help
themselves to dry grain.   If they do not run on
grass, give them all the fine chopped green food
they will eat.

About the best way to feed dry grain is have two
boxes, one large low box with about one inch of chaff
or finely cut hay or straw for scratching box, and one
box made as follows: For 100 chicks make a box 3
feet long V shape; one side $\frac{1}{2}$ inch lumber $3\frac{1}{2}$ inches
wide, front side a strip of tin or zinc $2\frac{1}{2}$ inches wide.
Turn over upon edge so the metal will not injure
them, nail the metal to the edge of the board—place
a division in the box for two kinds of grain, and cover
with glass with the corners ground off, leaving sufficient space for their heads to pass in under the glass.
Keep each division of this box full of dry grain.   If
you feed but two kinds of dry grain, fill the feed box
with one kind and throw a few handfuls of the other
kind in the scratch box once or twice a day; if you
feed 3 kinds, keep 2 kinds in the feed box: if you
use 4 kinds give them a change in their scratch box
and feed box.   Cracked corn should be sifted before
throwing in the scratching box; the fine meal given
in their soft food.

The object in giving them soft food in the morning is, their craws are empty and they are hungry
and the soft food will more readily relieve their
hunger and prevent them from gorging themselves
with dry grain.   When they become accustomed to
having dry grain by them continually, if they have

their soft food in the morning they will not eat any more dry grain than they require. The kind of grain which may be fed sparingly they will scratch hard for in their scratching box. Make a box similar to feed box with 3 divisions for coarse sand, bone meal and charcoal, and give them clear, fresh water in fountains. Keep their runs clean and give them good dusting material and a warm place to go to when they are cold.

We have Langshan that weighed $3\frac{3}{4}$ ℔s. each when 14 weeks old. We find our chicks do well on the above method of feeding.

BUSINESS NOTES.

No questions answered except on receipt of a cash order, or two 2 cent stamps. It is enough for me to give my time, without furnishing stamps and stationery.

Two stamps would be a trifle to you, yet it would not cover the cost to me as I did not make allowance in my prices for this expense. I cannot give my time to writing letters at my own expense. The way letters of inquiry have been coming in, in proportion to the orders, I should have at least $1.50 more for the Regulators to cover this unnecessary expense. You are at liberty to manufacture anything described in this book except the Regulator and Egg Turner.

Patents granted on Egg Turner, Oct. 31st, 1887. On Incubator Heat Regulator, Jan. 5, 1888. 1 intend to protect my rights.

By Nov. 1, 1888, I will complete an illustrated work entitled, "The Honest Poultryman's Companion," devoted more especially to the mechanical branch of the business. (I would state, however, the branch of the poultry business in which I am at times the most deeply interested is picking the bones).

My book will show a practical way by which seven or eight Brooders can be arranged to accommodate 1,000 chicks or less, and supply each with an abundance of fresh, warm air, and dispose of the carbonic acid gas; at the same time giving each Brooder any degree of heat desired.   All regulated to a different degree of heat with one Regulator.

It will be more thorough on important points, simply referred to in this book.   It will be neatly bound, printed on good paper and contain much valuable information not easily obtained.   Should you want this book let me know soon by postal card and I will notify you when the books are ready. Price, 50 cts.   Otherwise, should this book meet with no better success than my first the third will never go to press.

RECAPITULATION.

Zinc will answer in place of tin and paper as described on page 9.   It is also better for ventilator and heater tubes than tin, as it will not rust.

The heated air, in circulating hot-water Incubators (for regulating the heat) may be taken from the top and center of the heater box.

For No. 00 and No. 000 Incubators, a wood chimney placed on the back or side of the heater is just as good as the tin tubes for regulating purposes. Make the top square so the valve cap will fit inside, cover the top with a small board; cut a round hole in the cover to fit in valve cap.   Lower opening for hot air to enter should be from 1x5 to 1x6 inches in the clear.

One lamp will do for the 150 egg Incubator, No. 00, if it is placed in the center on the back of the Incubator.

The heater tubes should then be arranged the same as the 130 egg Incubator, No. 000. No. 1 drawer is 30 inches wide inside and holds 12 eggs in each row. No, 0 drawer is 25 inches wide and holds 10 eggs to the row. Should you want a drawer to hold more or less eggs to the row, allow $2\frac{1}{2}$ inches in width for each row. $4\frac{3}{4}$ inches in height will do as well as 5 inches for drawer. $1\frac{1}{4}$ inches between upper edge of the drawer and the bottom of the heater will do as well as 1 inch and will give more space for regulator tubes. Hard pine makes good drawers.

In constructing a different Incubator from No. 1, if you will be governed by the plans for constructing No. 1 and make the necessary difference in measurement and note the change as specified, you will have no difficulty in constructing any Incubator mentioned in this book.

My Regulators and Turners are a decided improvement to the Poultry Keeper and Common Sense Incubators. A good way to order a Regulator and Turner is to order a drawer complete; the drawers are very cheap.

The only practical way by which the heat can be successfully regulated, to obviate the outside and lamp changes of temperature in an Incubator, is by means of a machine that will regulate the heat by the *heat*, in the egg chamber. My machine will do this.

Valve caps will be made to fit over valve cups or pipes of the following sizes:

No. 000, capacity 130 eggs, diameter of cap 2¼ inches.

"	00	"	150	"	"	"	2½	"
"	0	"	200	"	"	"	2⅝	"
"	1	"	240	"	"	"	3	"
"	2	"	400	"	"	"	3½	"
"	3	"	600	"	"	"	4	"
"	4	"	800	"	"	"	5	"
"	6	"	1200	"	"	"	6¼	"
"	8	"	1600	"	"	"	7	"

No. 3 and No. 4 caps will cost 25 cents extra.
No. 6 and No. 8 "   "   50 "   "

TESTIMONIALS.

Mr. Hile forwarded to me a Regulator for experiment, but which arrived too late to test before he issued his book. I can easily see, from my experience, that it will be a valuable acquisition to those contemplating the construction of an Incubator, and it is a surprise that some one had not thought of the plan before. In a future number of the *Poultry Keeper* my results will be published, and I have no doubt they will be very favorable.   P. H. JACOBS, *Ed. Poultry Keeper.*

[When Mr. Jacobs tests the Egg Turner in connection with my improved drawer, he will see another point that will make him wonder some one had not thought of it before. Mr. Jacobs, editor of the *Poultry Keeper*, published in Parksburg. Pa., is well known by over 100,000 readers of his journal, as being a man, who, in defense of right and justice, recognizes or fears neither friend nor foe, when they oppose him.]

MR. HILE, *Dear Sir*: Being a breeder of Fancy Poultry, and having had considerable experience with Incubators, I do not hesitate to state emphatically that your Incubator Heat Regulators and Turners are not equaled in this country, and that your Incubators are not surpassed. In all, they make the most practical Incubator in use.   W. B. McCoY.
Valley Falls, Kan.

MR. HILE, *Dear Sir:* I built an Incubator last spring after your plan, and purchased your Egg Turner and Heat Regulator. I do not think they can be beaten. I believe I can beat the best hen in America hatching chickens. Enclosed is 25 cents for Moisture Guage.

Respectfully, P. J. TOBY.
W. W. Junction, Wis.

[Mr. Toby is a reliable breeder of Langshans, R. C. W. Leghorns and Mammoth Bronze Turkeys.]

MR. HILE: Having seen one of your Incubators in operation I am satisfied it is just what I want to hatch my Plymouth Rock, Light Brahma and White Leghorn eggs in. My eggs are too valuable to spoil in a snide Incubator. Your Regulator works to perfection. Let me know your price of a No. 1 Incubator without outside casing. Yours truly, F. C. HARWOOD.
South Cedar, Kan.

MR. HILE: Your Regulator and Turner received. I do not see why some men have doubts about their working; any man with any brains can see through it at a glance, so simple and yet so correct. I have tested it, and would never run another Incubator without one of your Regulators and Turners. I made a drawer after plans in your book, and it is another one of the best things I ever saw. I would not take anything for that book if I could not get another. You can put my name down for your coming book; let me know when it will be ready. Enclosed is 25 cents for Moisture Guage; I know it is just like the rest of your things. If your inventions please everybody like they do me, you are bound for the top of the ladder if you are not there already. Yours truly, W. E. HUMPHREYVILLE.
Houston, Tex.

J. W. HILE: You can say for C. B. Cage, that your Regulator and Turner takes the cake, baker and all. It is money thrown away to buy most any of the patent machines. I have one after your plan, boiler and pipes. The Regulator works as fine as $\frac{1}{2}$ degree. I have seen most all kinds and would not exchange my *machine for any* of them. You can say for *me* in language as strong as you please, that your *inventions* are *perfect* and *entirely reliable* and are the *only ones* I have ever seen that are *safe* and *sure*. CHAS. B. CAGE.
Shelbyville, Ind.

[Mr. Cage is well known as a prominent breeder and as a man of integrity; the Wyandott prize winner.]

MR. HILE: I built a Hot Air Incubator after the plans in your book and it works perfectly. I have been trying for some time to get a good practical Incubator and find that yours fills the bill exactly.

Yours truly,   E. H. McARTHUR.

Meridian, Miss.

[Mr. McArthur publishes the *Southern Poultry Guide*, price, 50 cts. It is an excellent journal and keeper up with the times. Send for a copy.]

LATEST IMPROVEMENTS.

By making the drawers $4\frac{1}{4}$ inches high outside (this will leave them $2\frac{3}{4}$ inches deep inside) and by making the ventilator box $\frac{3}{4}$ of an inch narrower, or by raising the heater box $1\frac{1}{2}$ inches to give $2\frac{1}{2}$ inches space between the bottom of the heater and the top of the egg drawer, I can furnish regulators to fit in this space to regulate lamp flames of from one to four lamps to one Incubator.

In ordering lamp regulators give exact measurement of this space, and state which way the drawer slides in, and the thickness of the walls.

These regulators will work in any Incubator having $2\frac{1}{4}$ inches space or more between the drawer and the heater. They are absolutely reliable and *cannot get out of order*. Price for one lamp Incubator, boxed, $5.00, 25 cents extra for each additional lamp attchments, for common or any kind of lamps.

In starting an Incubator, the regulators should not be connected with the lamps until the heat is up to the required degree inside. Otherwise, as the heat would rise, the flame would be turned down, and make it difficult to raise the heat inside.

The following dimensions are sufficient for Incubators with these regulators. Heater box, $5\frac{1}{2}$ inches deep, inside; space for regulator $2\frac{1}{2}$ to $2\frac{1}{4}$ inches. Ventilator box 6 inches inside; drawer $4\frac{3}{4}$ outside; space for sawdust for walls 4 to 5 inches; space for sawdust on top of heater 8 inches. The drawers may also be made of thinner lumber. Otherwise, they should be made the same as described, except the tubes should be shorter in proportion. Short lamp tubes, should have tin above the tube inside of the heater to guard against fire.

These Incubators can be taken through an ordinary door. The drawer regulators, regulate the heat by opening and closing a valve to let the heat pass out of the egg chamber or heater box. They are not practically adapted to regulate the heat by raising and lowering the lamp flame.

Lamp Regulators will operate a valve as well as lamp flame, or both at the same time. You are at liberty to manufacture my Incubators for your own use, but not for the market. Authorized manufacturers are

J. L. Wilson, Orangeville, Ill.

Frank Knowles, Little Hocking, Ohio.

J. W. Hile, Valley Falls, Kan.

Prices are reasonable. There will be a slight difference in prices owing to the variations in price of lumber, yet it will pay to order from the nearest factory. The Incubators are made to work in harmony with science and philosophy. Parties wanting Regulators and Turners should order of me.

PRICES OF LAMP INCUBATORS AND SUPPLIES.

It will be noticed I have made a reduction in my prices of Regulators and Egg Turners. My present facilities for manufacturing have permitted me to do so.

No. 1 Hot Water, complete, capacity, 240 eggs, $36.00
"   0 "   "   "   "   200 "   32.00
"   00 "   "   "   "   150 "   28.00
" 000 "   "   "   "   130 "   26.00
For Circulating Hot Water Incubators, same capacity, add 10 per cent. to the above prices.
No. I Hot Air, complete, capacity, 240 eggs,   30.00
"   0 "   "   "   "   200 "   28.00
"   00 "   "   "   "   150 "   26.00
" 000 "   "   "   "   130 "   25.00
Valve Regulators boxed for shipping, $5.25
Lamp   "   "   "   "   for one lamp, $5.00
25 cents extra for each additional lamp attachments.
Egg Turners, capacity, 240 or upwards. $2.25
"   "   "   under 240 to 200   2.00
"   "   "   "   200 to 150   1.75
"   "   "   "   150 to 100   1.50
Egg Drawers, No. 1, $2.25; No. 0, $2.00; No. 00, $1.75;
No. 000, $1.50.
Incubator Lamps, each,   65 cents.
"   "   Elbows, each,   30   "
Zinc Moisture Pans, per 50 square inches,   15   "
"   Heater Tubes, 18 to 20 inches long, each, 12½ "
"   Ventilator Tubes with caps,   6   "
Moisture Guages, post-paid,   25   "
Thermometers,   "   75   "
Carbonic Acid Gas Tubes, each,   15   "

These tubes are a decided improvement to any Incubator, if they run from under the egg drawer as
described on page 10.

In ordering Incubators or Regulators, state the
kind of Regulator you want. If Lamp Regulators,
state the sides the lamps are on and the distance
they are from each corner. For Lamp Incubator
Lamp Regulators are preferable. For Poultry Keeper, Farm and Garden and Scientific American Incubators (without lamps) the Valve Regulators are
used.   J. W. HILE,
Valley Falls, Kansas.